Mortymer House

A Novella

By

Meryl M Williams

The author Meryl M Williams b 1966

Meryl was born in South Wales and worked in the field of medical research before publishing a selection of poetry anthologies now followed by this, her third novella. This new work was extensively researched using the excellent facilities of Meryl's local library. She would like to extend her thanks to the library staff and to the Bath Chronicle for providing all the information contained respecting war time life in her area.

BY THE SAME AUTHOR

Poetry
Mementoes in Verse
Reflections of Time
Doodles, Dog Ears and Ditties
A Boy's Anthem
Moods in Bloom

Andrew's Amazing Odyssey and Other Stories

Novellas
The Judge Jones Trilogy
My Lady's Sovereign

MORTYMER HOUSE

Contents List

Chapter 1

Sir Arnold Steps In

The clock chimed the hour and dark clouds obscured the moon. A chill wind sprang up and Rosemary looked up to feel the first few drops of rain on her weary face. It was midnight and Edward, Earl of Ramptonshire was late for the first time. Their young baby lay sleeping in a wicker basket at her feet and she moved the makeshift cradle into the church porch out of the rain. Edward was never normally late for one of their rendezvous and unless he'd had an accident or his horse had shed a shoe, she must face the possibility that he wasn't going to show up.

Edward had been full of empty and broken promises. He said he would take her to France where they would secretly marry, then he said that would be impossible as it would give rise to his being disinherited by his formidable mother. He would keep her at Lindley Hall as a cook and have the baby brought up on the estate. Finally, he promised to take the child to his lands north of the border where a childless couple in one of his cottages would bring the baby up as their own. Empty promises, broken dreams, and at midnight outside the church of St Jude's

Rosemary wept for the sleeping infant who had as yet no name.

Rosemary was a farmer's daughter and she had worked the land from an early age. Then she caught the attention of the young Earl when he was out riding with his steward. She had loved him dearly but he was promised from birth to his wealthy distant cousin who had lands adjoining his in Scotland. Mary of Stirling was reputed to be beautiful as well as rich and said to be descended from an ancient royal house. No, Rosemary could never aspire to marry the Earl of Ramptonshire but he had promised to do his best by his son. He had agreed to meet them at the door of St Jude's at sundown on Easter Eve and by a quarter past midnight it was clear he wasn't coming.

The clock chimed the half hour as Rosemary stood up from bending over the sleeping baby, holding him for one last time, bestowing a final kiss and wrapping him more snuggly in her old shawl. She left the baby in his basket in the church porch, uttering a quiet prayer that some kind soul would take pity on her child, then she turned away to start the long walk back to Munros Farm, through the deserted graveyard and out into the open countryside. The farm where Rosemary had lived all her life was five miles from the nearest habitation and the rain came down, soaking the young mother to the skin.

The bells rang out for Easter Day and the verger, coming to unlock the church for morning prayer, found the baby boy now awake, hungry and wailing. The Rector was alerted and a local parishioner knocked at the door of the neighbourhood constable who began a concerted search for the missing mother with all the men of Feverfew village and nearby Scatterton. Messengers were sent to Lindley Hall where the young Earl was found to have left for London. At Mortymer House, the nurse Miss Irene Flotsam heard the story from the chambermaid and told Sir Arnold as she gave him his morning shave.

Sir Arnold's heart was moved by the story and he sent men from his estate to help in the search for the missing young woman. Meanwhile he asked Miss Flotsam to take a walk to the house where a matron was caring for the abandoned baby, and the Baronet offered support and financial aid. Mrs Toogood had named the baby Rupert but shook her head, saying she wondered what would become of him as she had four promising children of her own. Miss Flotsam held Rupert in her arms and wondered as women have for centuries why this timeless, ageless scenario should happen again and again. The two ladies talked about the search for Rupert's mother but wondered and exclaimed over whether she would be found alive.

Sir Arnold Chepstow had fought bravely in the trenches of the Great War but sustained severe injuries. He had come home to Mortymer House and lived quietly with Miss Flotsam his nurse and companion; she was a little older than the Baronet and had some experience of nursing military personnel at the National Military Hospital in neighbouring Thatchford, a town of considerable size ten miles south of Feverfew. Irene Flotsam was popular with Sir Arnold and his household as she was gentle and thoughtful. He would often recall that some of the other candidates he had interviewed had been a little too brisk. The nurse had a soft, contralto speaking voice that was easy on the ear, her long, blonde hair was tightly knotted in the French manner in a chignon and she wore a crisp, white uniform.

Two days after Sir Arnold had heard the news about the abandoned baby, he sat in his breakfast parlour gazing out of the windows at the avenue of conifers in his grounds and he felt helpless at being unable to assist in the search for the missing young woman. Feeling hampered by his injured legs, confined to his chair, he pondered in his heart if there was any way out of this ghastly mess. He thought about his great grandfather's duelling pistols on display in the study and wondered should he turn them on himself?

Sir Arnold's gloomy thoughts were interrupted by the Butler tapping gently on the door to announce the arrival of the Feverfew village constable. Kindly Constable Pendlebury stood before the Baronet and sadly shook his head.

"We have found the body of a young woman Sir", he said, "she is believed to be a Miss Rosemary Munro who was reported missing by her parents two days ago. Mr Munro was distraught when he came into Feverfew village to see me. It seems the young lady had got herself into a spot of trouble and her father had words. He says he doesn't know who the father of the child is but someone working on the farm says she had often been seen in the company of the young Earl. The Earl of Ramptonshire is their landlord but he was found to have left for London. Mr Munro is riding into Thatchford this week to try and identify his only daughter, who currently rests at the undertaker's chapel".

"It's a terrible tragedy", was Sir Arnold's dignified response. "We must make every effort to contact the Earl. Have we any news as to when he might return?"

"It's bad news I'm afraid Sir", said the constable, "the Earl has gone to London for the summer and expects to return to his lands North of the border afterwards. We have no proof that he is the father but the Rector of Lindley Parish will send a letter craving His Grace's assistance. Mrs Toogood is taking care of the baby but we are all concerned as to the boy's future".

"Constable Pendlebury you have been more than helpful and I know that you are doing all you can. If we find the father and if he will not take responsibility let young Rupert come to Mortymer House. I will speak to my solicitor in Thatchford to see how we are placed. I have sent Mrs Toogood some financial aid but she has four promising children of her own. I can afford a nurse and to send the child to a good, local school. Let the Rector of Lindley wait upon me and I will speak with him".

"Very good Sir Arnold", replied the constable and bowing his head he left to go back to Feverfew village.

Chapter 2

Rupert's Great Adventure

Mortymer House stood on higher ground, in a beautiful parkland of immaculately kept verdant grass with noble horse chestnut trees and a new avenue of conifers leading to the magnificent front entrance. The building was of fine, cream sandstone with high gables and narrow windows with old fashioned leaded frames. The house had been in the Chepstow family for four generations having been purchased by Sir Arnold's great-grandfather old Sir Malcolm Chepstow on acquiring his title for services to the realm. Sir Arnold had meant to make improvements to the grounds and kitchen gardens and had succeeded in restoring the magnificent formal gardens where he would sit for many hours in the summer, Miss Flotsam by his side reading aloud.

These formal gardens were now extremely well cared for and were the pride of the county. There were daffodils and tulips in the spring, roses in the summer then chrysanthemums in the autumn. In winter, Sir Arnold liked to sit looking out over the parkland from his ground floor study when the branches of the trees were bare and he could see right across the valley to the Welsh border. The dark, almost menacing Brecon Beacons on the far horizon seemed at times a challenge. His secret dream was to go there, to fling himself out of this accursed chair and just walk, walk for miles with just a stick, water and a packed lunch.

He was roused from his almost ferocious longings by a tap on the door. It was his Butler announcing that the Rector of St Mary's church was in the morning room. Sir Arnold was of slim build and a featherweight so with assistance from Martin his faithful servant he was able to use his arms to move his body into the wheeled chair that was kept near him at all times. Martin pushed the chair gently along to the morning room where the vicar awaited them and there, somewhat to their surprise, was Mrs Toogood holding baby Rupert in her arms.

"Sir Arnold", cried the Rector in his booming, bass voice, "how good of you to take in this poor, abandoned baby. It seems that Miss Munro had got into a spot of trouble and so far no-one in the area has laid claim to the boy. Freddy Toogood has seen Miss Munro in the company of the Earl of Ramptonshire but his Grace says he is not responsible for the child. The grandparents have declared they are too busy with farming to look after the child properly so they, as the child's only surviving next of kin, have given full permission to you to adopt baby Rupert". Mrs Toogood gently placed the baby boy into Sir Arnold's outstretched arms as she spoke of the sad death of the little one's mama. She was pleased to see that Sir Arnold took to the child at once, kissing Rupert on the forehead then admiring the baby's tiny hands and feet.

"We will give him into the care of Miss Sally Anne, an experienced nursery nurse from Feverfew Village, while Miss Flotsam and I will always be on hand to guide and supervise his upbringing. We will wait until he is quite grown before telling him of his challenging start in life but he seems robust and should thrive here at Mortymer House. He will be well provided for and if I can adopt him legally he will be my heir, then I will have a son to whom I can leave all I possess including my title which was so hard won by old Sir Malcolm." Smiling, he looked up at the portraits of his great grandparents above the mantelpiece, then he rang the bell for Miss Sally Anne, tenderly handing over to her this most precious charge. The Rector of St Mary's then shook Sir Arnold's hand, thanked him warmly and departed, taking Mrs Toogood with him home to Feverfew Village.

Chapter 3

A Countess Comes to Call

One chilly autumn morning when mists appeared to rise from the grass while the raw dampness got into your bones, Miss Flotsam visited Rupert in the nursery where he was engrossed in his breakfast.

"How is he getting on Sally Anne?" Irene asked the nursery maid who was stoking up the fire and putting the kettle on for a morning cup of tea.

"Well he has fine and lusty lungs", answered Sally Anne proudly as she gave the fire one final poke. Miss Flotsam moved to the window to see if the mist would clear enough for Sir Arnold to take a turn around the park in his motorised chair. The windows of the nursery looked out onto the sweeping drive of Mortymer House and as Miss Flotsam stood at the window she saw a fine, expensive motor car pull up before the main entrance below. A uniformed chauffeur stood up from the driver's seat and opened the passenger door for his employer, a tall, willowy young woman wearing an elegant coat with a long cigarette holder in her gloved right hand. The housekeeper was at the door to greet this unexpected visitor and the fine lady was admitted to the house where she was shown into the drawing room to await Sir Arnold as he rose hastily from his breakfast.

When Sir Arnold entered the drawing room, the visitor was at the window, looking out on the lawn and formal gardens. She turned to speak, saying quite softly but distinctly, "Sir Arnold I am Mary of Ramptonshire. I understand that you are holding my husband's child".

"Your Grace, won't you sit down?" Sir Arnold asked her from his wheeled chair.

"I must apologise, I am unable to rise", he insisted. Mary noticed for the first time that Sir Arnold had been badly wounded in the Great War.

"Sir Arnold", she said, extending her hand, "I am unable to have a child and we would like to raise my husband's offspring as our own. I have money, I will pay you well. You will have the finest London doctors, the latest treatments. You could see Europe, take the Spa waters. All this will I give you if you will only let me have the child. After all, what is the child to you?" She spoke breathlessly and with much passion but Sir Arnold, although deeply moved, remained firm. Rupert was now an important part of life at Mortymer House, the baronet looked forward to greeting him every day so, rising to this sudden and new threat, Sir Arnold also spoke with passion.

"I have adopted Rupert Chepstow as my own. The child was abandoned by his parents then his poor, poor

11

mother was found dead. The maternal grandparents were unable to take the child so as Rupert's natural guardians they gave permission to me to adopt the child. I have legal papers, your Grace, Rupert is my son and heir. I too am unable to have a child."

Mary stood up and again looked out at the formal gardens with their topiary and immaculate box hedges.

"Sir Arnold, my husband is distraught at losing his son. He speaks constantly of having a child, might I see the boy?"

"Your Grace", said Sir Arnold firmly, "at the time the boy was found, cold, lonely and abandoned in the church porch, the local constable made every effort to contact the Earl. The Rector also called at Lindley Hall, then sent messages to London and to Ramptonshire. Eventually we heard that your husband felt he had no claim to the boy and gave me his blessing to take him in. How would I ever trust the Earl to take care of his son if this is the start in life he gave him?".

Mary of Stirling had been twenty five years old on her marriage to the Earl of Ramptonshire and the ceremony took place at the family church near his parents home. The young couple honeymooned in Paris and Vienna but when they returned to Edward's London home he finally told her about Rosemary Munro and her abandoned baby. Mary was grieved in her heart but, being human, felt a certain degree of relief that the woman was dead. Two years passed as Edward and Mary longed for a child but there was no sign of any pregnancy. The Earl was eager to have an heir but in front of his mother he spoke bravely, saying that they were not yet ready for the responsibility. When he was alone with Mary he would reproach her then have a drink.

Mary did not consult her husband before setting out on the long journey to Feverfew Village, taking just her chauffeur and personal maid; she stayed two nights at the Crown Hotel, Thatchford. She heard many good reports of young Rupert and the care he was receiving from the baronet whose entire household had come to life once again. Mary's appeal to Sir Arnold had failed, she did not get to see the child so she returned to London to confess to her husband. Edward poured himself a whiskey and soda then glared at her.

"It was very brave of you", he declared, "I admit I was always surprised when Chepstow took it into his head to adopt a by-blow like that but he will do it proud, war hero and all that with the community on his side. But I forbid you to approach him again."

Mary walked from the house the next morning, walking in the rain through Kensington Gardens and sitting dismally under a tree to consider her fate. She felt lost and unable to love her husband at that moment. He had a proven record of success, he seemed to have no doubt that Rupert Chepstow was his, so Mary formed the resolute plan of visiting a Harley Street specialist and then she argued with herself, she must get Edward to do the same.

Dr Jetsam was kind and a little old-fashioned. He examined the Countess, asking seemingly pointless questions, but assured her he found nothing wrong. He felt sure the child would come suggesting to his patient that she might like to try some new activities.

"Could you learn to type or stitch kneelers for the church?" He queried after shaking his head over how she whiled away her time. "Do something to take your mind off the worry, don't sit at home thinking about it too much. Help the poor, visit the countryside or ask the Earl to take you to Brighton for some sea air, it might be just what you need".

Mary spoke to Edward that evening but he lost his temper and refused to meet with Dr Jetsam.

"Wait, wait, wait, is that all he can say?" Edward paced around their new style lounge and reached for a stiff drink. "I can't see the point of visiting the doctor."

Mary did not have the courage to persist, she contemplated consulting her mother in law but then decided to speak with the local vicar's wife; after all she had nothing to lose. Mrs Trill was a very slight, lively, young woman who darted like quicksilver around her lounge as she brought out examples of fine needlecraft to show the Countess.

"Your Grace, have you done much stitching before?" The vicar's wife was very keen to help and being a mother of a large brood herself understood that for Mary the wait was taxing to her health.

"Yes indeed I have, before my marriage", answered Mary, touched by Mrs Trill's warmth and womanly bonding. "Since I married the Earl I have stitched a little but find it hard to come up with ideas. I made a hanging for Edward's study showing his favourite view of Loch Lomond and he liked it very much".

"You sound very skilled", said Mrs Trill "where would you like to start? Perhaps if you did some traditional kneelers then in time for next year we will be working on a frontal for our High Altar. We have a number of designs that we work on but once you've gained some experience you will be designing your own".

Mary returned to her home light of heart but found that Edward had departed for his club and was not expected home until late that night. The following morning the damp set in with a steady drizzle so typical of London weather, so after a brisk walk in Hyde Park Mary decided to make a start on her kneelers. She was very soon absorbed in her work then Edward came downstairs for a late breakfast.

"Mary, it looks very nice. Can I commission some for the chapel at Lindley Hall? I was going to sell the old morgue, it needs money spent on it badly, but what say you we go there next summer? I'll have the house and gardens cleaned up and the dust sheets thrown off. Why I might even have a shot at clay pigeons". Mary was thrilled and proud that he had suggested the idea, she felt that the country air would do them both good and maybe Edward would spend less time drinking.

Chapter 4

Taking Tea at Mortymer House

Rupert Chepstow started at the local village school in Feverfew coming home each day to chat to his guardian and Miss Flotsam about all his friends and pursuits. He showed promise from an early age, bringing home good reports from the school masters. Christmas that year was celebrated quietly at their family home at Mortymer House and two friends of Sir Arnold's from his time in the army came to stay for a few weeks. At times such as these, Miss Flotsam stayed more in the background but she liked Major John Parry and his young wife Geraldine and was sometimes invited to join Mrs Parry in the morning room while the Major and his host discussed the morning papers in Sir Arnold's study. That year they all awoke on New year's Day to a landscape shrouded in white as heavy snow had fallen across the valley and on the surrounding hillsides. Major and Mrs Parry could not get the railway train back to London for two days until the line was cleared. Rupert enjoyed the weather of course, building a big snowman in the middle of the lawn and throwing snowballs at the stable hands as they took the horses out for exercise. At this time Sir Arnold was at his happiest, his sombre moments in the days before Rupert came into their lives were all forgotten. Miss Flotsam noticed how changed he was but never ceased to work and hope, dreaming that as Rupert grew then the baronet would one day leave his chair and walk again.

When Rupert reached his sixth birthday, coinciding with another early Easter, Miss Flotsam organised a birthday party for him and all his schoolmates. The corridors of Mortymer House echoed with the sound of laughter and little feet for the first time since Sir Arnold was a boy. Some days later, on a glorious sunny day as winter slowly gave way to spring, Rupert was in school as Sir Arnold was in his study. Miss Flotsam approached her overlord to enquire after his health but the baronet was not in the best of humours as his solicitors at Thatchford had been approached by the Earl of Ramptonshire himself.

"Yes Miss Flotsam?" He greeted her, "is something troubling you?"

"Sir Arnold", said Miss Flotsam, somewhat nervously, "Feverfew and our neighbours at Scatterton have a new doctor. He is freshly trained in London with new ideas and his name is Dr Shiraz. I have heard nothing but good reports of him and wondered would you see him?"

"Yes I will, it will relieve the monotony of life at Mortymer House", answered Sir Arnold.

"Miss Flotsam, may we take tea?"

"Sir Arnold", she asked, concerned, "have you had bad news?"

"The Earl of Ramptonshire wants Rupert, I admit I am bothered after all Edward is hale and hearty and could have another. I don't know why he keeps pestering us."

"Sir Arnold", his nurse asked, "could somebody else have been Rupert's father?"

"Irene, we will take tea. Ring the bell."

The butler brought the tea pot, hot water, cups and saucers setting them out on the small table at Sir Arnold's elbow. He enquired if Sir would take a muffin but Sir Arnold had lost all his appetite. Miss Flotsam poured the tea for him and added a lump of sugar while Sir Arnold was lost in his own thoughts. Finally the baronet spoke.

"Irene, I have received many concerned letters from friends I knew before the war, friends who have been kind to me and never failed to keep in touch. They tell me that Edward, Earl of Ramptonshire, has plans to sell Lindley Hall to pay off gambling debts and I also hear that his drinking is worse than ever. My closest friend Major John Parry has met the Countess of Ramptonshire through Mrs Parry's work with the Women's Institute. She will see no wrong in her husband's worrying behaviour but Geraldine Parry did not feel able to ask too many questions. But dearest Irene, could it be that you have reason to suggest that the Earl is not Rupert's birth father?"

"Well, rumours are nothing new to Feverfew", said Miss Flotsam, "but Thomas Brakespeare is now confiding in Freddy Toogood that there were other men seen with Rosemary Munro. We have no proof it was the Earl and sadly Miss Munro is not here to speak for herself."

"Yet the Earl of Ramptonshire himself has finally laid claim to the boy and threatens legal action to have Rupert removed to London. The Earl expresses dissatisfaction that Rupert attends a so-called common village school. Edward insists he can give his son a better start in life."

"He doesn't have a leg to stand on", answered Miss Flotsam, "especially with drink and gambling problems".

"Dearest Miss Flotsam, did you never think to get married and have children of your own?"

"Sir Arnold, I am married to my job", replied the redoubtable nurse, "and I would find it very hard to leave you now".

"Irene, tell me about Dr Shiraz. Have you met him?"

Chapter 5

A Recovery Launched

Doctor Shiraz was freshly qualified after a rigorous training in London. He had chosen a country practice to bring up his young family away from the smog, noise and dust of the big city. He was brimming with new ideas, full of optimism and enthusiasm said Miss Flotsam so she was sure it was worth a try.

The appointment was made initially for the new doctor to attend on Sir Arnold at the morning room of Mortymer House. The baronet fidgeted nervously with his tie as he began to itch with impatience then the good doctor was ushered in by Martin, Sir Arnold's faithful butler.

"Dr Shiraz, forgive me for not rising", said Sir Arnold, extending his right hand. The doctor shook hands with a warm, comforting grip then sat down at the baronet's invitation. Dr Shiraz spoke with a gentle, slightly womanish voice beginning by asking how Sir Arnold had come by his injuries. The patient fidgeted with his tie once again and avoided the doctor's firm stare.

"You see doctor", he finally admitted, "I never speak of it".

The doctor leaned back a little in his chair and crossed his legs.

"Sir Arnold, I have read your medical notes held at the National Military Hospital here at Thatchford but there is no account of your personal experiences. Would you be able to remember at all or is it really too painful?"

Sir Arnold looked out of the window at his immaculate, formal gardens as he heard once again the shelling all around him. He felt the weight of his comrade at arms slump against him as George Raymond was hit. Then he felt the searing pain and the cold, wet mud as he too went down. The shelling ceased for a while then the stretcher lifted Sir Arnold out of the trenches. There was a nurse at Thatchford who spent long hours encouraging him to eat again, then the long days and lonely nights. Finally the trip home to Feverfew and worst of all, the compassionate faces of his house staff as his bedroom was made up downstairs.

"It's a funny thing Dr Shiraz", said Sir Arnold, looking up at last, "but no-one has ever asked me before".

The doctor explained that he needed to test his patient for stiffness which he did by examining the baronet's arm movements then he finished by testing Sir Arnold's reflexes using a small hammer. As the doctor lightly tapped his patient's knee the hammer elicited a tiny response.

"Tell me Sir Arnold, how does this feel?" Dr Shiraz asked as he brought the pointed handle of the hammer along the length of the baronet's foot.

"Dr Shiraz, I feel sensation but I cannot stand up much less walk."

"Sir Arnold as you are having to remain in your seat there is a danger you will gain weight then standing will be even more out of reach. First I must recommend a diet but then I would like you to come and see me at the military hospital. We now have a dedicated team of professionals specially trained at bringing life back to injured legs. Will you work with me?"

"Doctor, I will try anything to get out of this chair. Give the details of the diet to my cook, we will collaborate with my nurse Miss Flotsam and I will instruct my chauffeur to take me to your clinic when the time comes".

Spring came to the grounds of Mortymer House with daffodils and primroses along the grass verges but Miss Flotsam was a little too excited to observe as the chauffeur brought Sir Arnold's motor car around the sweeping drive to take them both to Thatchford for treatment. It felt like a long, wearisome drive through the sleepy, country lanes then finally out onto the main road. Miss Flotsam sat in the backseat feeling nervous and edgy, wondering what would happen when they arrived at their destination. At the hospital, two kind orderlies in white uniforms assisted their new patient into a wheeled chair then moved him gently into a well lit waiting area. There were a few other patients some of whom could stand or even walk around as a number of smart nurses passed briskly by. Then Sir Arnold's name was called so he permitted his own nurse to push him into the large room where Dr Shiraz waited. The patient and his nurse were shown in to a very spacious room with long windows from floor to ceiling and a vast mirror against one inner wall. There were parallel bars near the mirror and the kind of leather horses associated with a gymnasium, not far from where Sir Arnold was placed there were also rings hanging from the high, oak beamed ceiling.

The doctor asked Sir Arnold a number of questions about his personal care. At first the patient hesitated, but the doctor's manner was one of calm reassurance so Sir Arnold relaxed as he spoke with accuracy about the difficulties of living with his condition.

"Sometimes I cope very well doctor", he explained, "but the winter months are the worst with the cold and damp making me feel as if every muscle aches. Yes I can feel my legs, I never forget they are there but they hang uselessly as my butler assists me to move from bed to chair and back again. I ordered a special upright bath to be made with a hinged door allowing me to move sideways onto a seat. In this way I can bathe myself, freeing my nurse from this rather more intimate service. She is a faithful, competent servant but one must preserve one's decency".

"It sounds like you cope admirably", exclaimed the good doctor, "how do you manage out of doors?"

"I try as far as is reasonably practicable to go out if weather permits. I have a motorised chair which I use to circumnavigate my estate and visit my tenants once the paths and driveway have been gravelled to make my passage smoother. The chair ambles along and Miss Flotsam often accompanies me or I talk to my agent. It's a difficult life but having Rupert around cheers us very much, he is always happy and bright as he makes friends with everybody. In a way I am glad we sent him to the local school as a day boy, I would be sorry to lose him to a boarding school miles from home".

Miss Flotsam bent down and spoke to Sir Arnold quietly.

"If you feel too much pain", she said, "we'll stop at once. The doctor is on hand together with Mr Charmouth should you fall. They will catch you safely, placing you straight back to your chair. I am on hand to take you straight home if you so wish but this young lady, Miss Lancelot, will serve you a fresh cup of tea once it's over. All you need to do is rise to your feet, supporting yourself by your arms, firmly grasping the parallel bars".

Sir Arnold nodded then, almost as an afterthought, removed his tie and undid his collar button. He leaned forward in his chair, gripping the parallel bars in a strong clasp to pull himself upright, then moved very gradually along the bars as his legs hung beneath him. He inched his way slowly, but surely, then sank gratefully back into his chair which was moved behind him by the practised Mr Charmouth. The kind doctor clapped the patient on the shoulder exclaiming his delight at this Sir Arnold's first attempt to propel himself.

"Very well done Sir Arnold", cried the whole team with one voice, then Miss Flotsam asked how her employer was feeling.

"A terrific sense of achievement", replied the baronet, "thank you Mr Charmouth. How often do we do this exercise?"

"If you can do this once a week to start with", said the quiet and unassuming male nurse, "then we will increase the intensity. Spend a little time at home thinking it through as mental rehearsal is often the key to success".

"Here comes the tea tray", announced a new face. It was Miss Lancelot asking should she pour and there was a selection of fruit.

After his session at the hospital Sir Arnold was much more cheerful. Once he and Miss Flotsam had returned to Mortymer House the baronet spoke to his ward to ask how Rupert had spent his day. The young lad brought paintings from his school that he had enjoyed making and also a plasticine model of his pony. The drawings were pinned to the wall of the baronet's study then Sir Arnold brought out a treasure box from a drawer in his desk. In the small oak box was a medal that Sir Arnold had won for bravery in the great war.

"You are young Rupert so I am showing you this to encourage you to grow up strong but gentle towards your fellow creatures. Do not wittingly harm anyone but live in love and charity with your neighbours". Then Sir Arnold told Rupert a bedtime story made up on the spot about a plasticine horse that came to life then escaped to the country. As darkness began to descend Sally Anne was called for, to take Rupert upstairs to bed.

"Miss Flotsam I feel a little celebration is in order so I have sent a glass of wine to your room. You must be exhausted after all the events of the day so take a day off tomorrow and I will manage with Martin".

"Very good Sir Arnold", and the nurse retired to her suite alongside her employer's on the ground floor although she felt much too excited to sleep after the day's events.

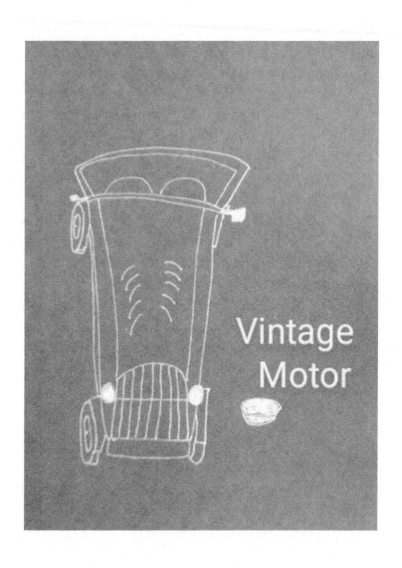

Vintage
Motor

Chapter 6

This Dreaming Idyll

April 1930 came in with balmy breezes as the gentle rains of spring refreshed the gardens. Miss Flotsam was preparing for a busy day in Thatchford to carry out a commission from Sir Arnold to purchase a draughts game for Rupert's eighth birthday and some new pocket handkerchiefs for the whole household. Also, she was to call in at the National Military Hospital to observe a demonstration of a newly invented stationary bicycle that could be operated with the arms. Dr Shiraz had asked her to view the new technology because he reasoned that to strengthen Sir Arnold's arm muscles would improve his stamina and allow him to propel himself more readily helping with his independence.

Mr Charmouth demonstrated the machine, explaining that it was safely grounded and unlikely to overturn even with quite vigorous arm movements. He spoke of improving muscle tone, showing with the help of a younger man from the wards how he could now propel his own chair at ground floor level without assistance once he was seated. Miss Flotsam wrote notes then after thanking the hospital staff she went out into the damp drizzle to make her purchases.

Sir Arnold followed his local newspaper the "Thatchford Observer" and Rupert was excited by the news of the new airship that was due to fly to Canada later that year in May. The young boy had asked if he could have the pig's bladder from his grandparents farm to make a balloon to which he would attach a balsa wood propellor attached with a rubber band. Sir Arnold secretly believed that the doomed project would never leave the ground but was absolutely forbidden from making any suggestion that the homemade version might not fly. Miss Flotsam bought the draughts set, was able to obtain some balsa wood from a model shop, then priced up the kits for making bi-planes which were also making the headlines.

When she returned home to Mortymer House she found Martin the butler waiting on the back stairs to speak with her.

"Sir Arnold is asking for you", said Martin, "something of a deep interest in the local newspaper". Miss Flotsam tapped gently at the study door then entered to find her employer making notes on his best cream wove paper.

"Ah yes, Miss Flotsam, cast your eye over the front page of today's Observer. Here a certain criminologist opposes the death sentence as he doesn't consider it to be a deterrent then there is the possibility they could hang the wrong man. I wonder what you think as I am writing a letter to my local Member of Parliament to call for this outdated practice to be abolished. After all, Irene it's just legalised murder. The gentleman addressing the House of Commons suggests that persons found not mentally responsible are being sentenced".

Miss Flotsam read the front page of the newspaper with great care then sat quietly for a moment as she considered her response.

"I am inclined to agree with you Sir Arnold", she said, "but genuinely thought I would not live to see it changed in our lifetimes".

"Well nurse, I really should type this letter on one of those new fangled machines but they are horribly expensive and have to be ordered from London. Could you support me learn how to use it?"

"Sir Arnold, may I just say how positive and wonderful it is to hear you take such an interest in current affairs. I am sure Lord Wayfayre would be heavily influenced by your point of view but even if he disagrees he may get other letters. I firmly believe he may listen, but see here there is a senior clergyman writes to say he wants the death penalty preserved because of blood thirsty quotes from the Old Testament."

"Well, I saw the vicar while you were at Thatchford but he was most careful not to express an opinion one way or the other. He spoke of forgiveness at length, but was rightly concerned that the victim's family should get justice. I see what he means by that but look at it another way Irene, I remember the agony of George Raymond being shot down in front of me but haven't sought to hang the soldier responsible. But then that was war and this is homicide and all we little people can do is write letters. Do you know how to order a typewriter? Would the big department store know?"

"Sir I will ask them next week, because I think the big police station in Sandmouth has one, Constable Pendlebury had seen it when he went there for extra training".

May came with sunny days after a morning dew as Miss Flotsam took breakfast with Sally Anne and Rupert before all three of them set off for the local village school. Sally Anne was chatty and they all were full of the news just announced from Sir Arnold that when Rupert was to start at the Thatchford Grammar School the young man would be presented with a bicycle.

"Rupert, we hear you are becoming musical and at Thatchford Grammar there is a fine school choir", Sally Anne announced as she went on to mention concerts and carol services at Christmas.

Miss Flotsam walked back to Mortymer House across the meadows then tapped on the door of Sir Arnold's study to enquire if she could be of service. Once again he was engrossed in the local newspaper.

"How do you fancy flying to Australia in under sixteen days, Miss Flotsam?" He held up the morning paper and she read about a famous woman aviator attempting to beat the world record.

"I would be terrified to go over the sea", replied Irene, "you see Sir Arnold I have never seen the sea but I hear it is so deep you can never get to the bottom, and so wide you can never see the other side".

"Miss Flotsam!" Cried Sir Arnold moving his wheeled chair closer towards her seat. " Why! There is sea at Sandmouth, a port and busy harbour. That's where they brought me home after I was injured. We will go there with Sally Anne before Rupert goes to grammar school, in the motor car with chauffeur. We can look out to sea while Rupert enjoys paddling in the shallows then you can bring me a shell or a pebble. I will be quite comfortable with the chauffeur." Miss Flotsam smiled in a little disbelief then suggested a turn in the formal gardens as it was such a lovely day. Then as May turned to June the local newspaper, The Thatchford Observer, reported that Prince George himself had come to open the new airport at far away Bristol so Sir Arnold was inspired to type a letter on his newly mastered machine, expressing all his hopes and dreams as his team built on his recovery.

Chapter 7

Welcoming New Life

That evening in his home in Kensington, London, Edward Earl of Ramptonshire sat down in his favourite armchair and leaned across to the small cabinet at his side. He groped for a moment, failed to find what he sought then Mary entered the room.

"Edward if you're looking for the whiskey it's all been poured down the sink". Edward slowly turned and glared at her.

"You really are very brave", he retorted, "Is there none in the house?"

"Not a drop", she answered, then she sat near him and took his hand. "Edward, in my own desperate and inimitable way I love you. I have just seen Dr Jetsam who gave me long awaited good news. Edward, I bear your child. Do you think that for the child's sake you would not have any more whiskey and speak to the doctor who may be able to help?"

Edward stood up and pulled her to her feet.

"Mary, I remember the day I achieved my majority at twenty one years old. They said I was intended for you and I never believed I could be so lucky. You are gracious, beautiful, rich and elegant, all the things that I am not. The day I made you mine I was nervous as a girl but is this really true what you are telling me? Are we indeed to have a child? Did the doctor do anything?" Mary laughed as she embraced her husband.

"The doctor merely advised patience so I had to learn to be patient with myself. The child will be the handsomest or prettiest and most loved child in Christendom. If we have a boy I would like to call him Edward and if she is a girl then Charlotte for Mrs Trill the vicar's wife who has sustained us through the years of waiting."

The Earl of Ramptonshire wanted to ask his blooming Countess if she would travel to the North for their baby's birth or if she would prefer to stop at their Kensington home. He ordered a special meal from the cook and changed his plans, making apologies to his club, deciding to dine at home.

"Here, I think", answered Mary "as it's cold and remote North of Glasgow where Rampton Towers is, especially in the winter. There are lots of advantages to staying in London, my Harley Street specialist is close by and there are good stores for baby things. We also have the gardens for exercise and it's expensive to transport the horses". In her heart Mary also knew that many of Edward's former drinking cronies would be spending Christmas and New

Year in Glasgow and they would all want to wet the baby's head.

Edward had once promised to take her to Lindley Hall but following Rosemary Munro's death and the abandoned son Rupert's adoption by Sir Arnold the Countess was not wanting to visit that area again or make any contact with this very dark part of Edward's past.

"Better to keep them apart", she thought to herself. But over dinner Edward had a surprise that was not so welcome.

"My aged parent, Mama, plans to make the trip to London in time for your lying in", declared Edward boldly.

"Oh dear!" Replied Mary, " won't the journey be too much for her?"

"It's her first grandchild", reproached the Earl, "she says she will come by motor car as she can't abide nasty, beastly steam trains. She is very resourceful and will be bringing her chauffeur as well as her chambermaid. There is plenty of space and I have asked the housekeeper to prepare the rooms; they will be here for three months."

Mary sighed and hastily wiped away a tear at this awful news, just hoping that her formidable mother-in-law would change her mind before the baby was due. Then, rallying, Mary changed the subject to speak at random of the planned christening and the robe she would be embroidering with white silk.

A large, bright blue motorcar pulled up in front of the Earl's house in Kensington and the chauffeur stepped out to open the passenger door for his employer the Dowager Countess. Edward greeted his mother with a somewhat stiff, formal handshake but then the older lady, in her long skirt that swept the gravel drive, paused to sum up her daughter-in-law.

"My dear you do look very well, pregnancy obviously suits you", she asserted, "but my what a journey. When did London get so busy? Well Mary I am overjoyed at the news of my first grandchild. I never told you before but I waited a long time to have Edward and then he had to be an only child. No reproach to you Mary, perhaps it's in our family. Well Edward, might we take tea?"

Mary's heart was warmed by this female bonding from her mama-in-law so she ordered hot, buttered muffins for tea with some of her very own plum butter and asked the older lady to preside. Afterwards, Mary left the Dowager to enjoy time with Edward while she herself went to inspect the developing nursery where the decorators had made pretty friezes of tropical fish around the fireplace. Mary unpacked a mobile of wooden and Papier mache animals that she hung in the large, casement window. Mary thought it looked amazing and was deeply touched when her mama-in-law was delighted with the room.

"It faces south-east so the baby will be woken by the sun", exclaimed the Dowager, "but my dear, Edward is completely transformed. What have you done?" Mary did not feel at all able to mention the whiskey bottles that she was still finding dotted around the house. She had asked the housekeeper not to order anymore and so far this plan was proving quite successful. But the Dowager was experienced and wise so tactfully she said nothing more but commented that her son would really enjoy being a father.

After dinner that evening the Dowager retired early as she was tired from her long journey. Edward spoke with Mary to ask her had it been as bad as she feared?

"No, she really is lovely", answered Mary, "but I never talk to you about my own parents as my father has died. But we believe my mother still lives, or at least have heard nothing to the contrary. My cousin had kept in touch even though the family shunned my mother for marrying beneath her. She lived in penury after the marriage then I was brought up by my father who always refused to talk on the matter. I do have in my possession a copy of their marriage certificate, I was born outside Stirling but my mother moved into the town".

"We must make every effort to trace them and also your aunt and uncle if they still live. Does your cousin still know them?" The Earl was suddenly amazed at the prospect of finding new in-laws and looked at his wife with a new respect.

"My cousin is as yet unmarried and lives with her parents so she certainly does know them", replied Mary, "but I did not hear from them on our marriage, only a short note of congratulations when I wrote about the new baby".

"In that case my love it is time to settle old scores. When the baby is born and you're fit to travel, we will visit them and see if the solicitor can trace your mother. If she is living in an impoverished manner she will be glad of some help and I'm sure she will want to see her grandchild".

Chapter 8

Grim Tidings

During the bright summer months of 1939, Miss Flotsam noticed that Sir Arnold was more than usually withdrawn. He chatted less as she assisted him and saw much less of her as he spent long hours talking with his agent Mr Rufus Cuthbert. Then after dinner he would retire early to take a cigar with Rupert on the patio. Little was said about it to the nurse but when she enquired if anything was needful Rupert gently took her to one side in the formal gardens.

"Miss Flotsam, news from Europe is ghastly, and not just Europe. The Japanese have attacked Soviet Forces on the Manchukuo Frontier where hostilities have erupted over the last six weeks. Closer to home, the Polish Government does not anticipate danger but the newspaper suggests that the Nazi threat is grave indeed. I may have to fight, but kind Sir Arnold is recommending that I finish my schooling so he won't let me sign up before I reach eighteen."

"Rupert, you were right to tell me, but I will do my best not to mention it too soon. I have not seen the newspaper for several weeks as Sir Arnold has kept the back copies I would normally look at when he's finished with them. If war is declared he will all but break his heart, you are the apple of his eye and if harm should come to you I don't know how we will cope."

"I will not be spared the horror that faces my fellow men", answered Rupert, "my much loved guardian has seen the worst that life can offer and although it was said that the Great War was the war to end all wars, it seems this threat from Europe is very real and must be faced. But Miss Flotsam, Sir Arnold is now asking for you so go to him with the care that I know you are very amply capable of." Then the young man left the house to go to see Tom Brakespeare who, although unable to read, had been speaking about having to fight after word reached Feverfew from Constable Pendlebury's wireless.

Miss Flotsam first went quietly down a long corridor towards the back of Mortymer House where the private chapel was lit with candles and an oil burning lamp. She looked in amazement at the stained glass behind the altar as if seeing it for the first time. The morning sun was pouring in, lighting up the window which gleamed, splashing the plain stone flagged floor with blues, greens and gold.

"Perhaps it will not come to war", she prayed earnestly, still standing before the coloured glass. Then she roused herself, straightened her uniform and approached Sir Arnold's study door.

"Irene", he called on hearing her knock, and she entered the neat, tidy room. She went up to his desk lightly touching his shoulder. He gripped her hand in his then in a very rare and touching gesture put it to his lips.

"Will you stay with me and read to me?" He asked and she agreed at once. "Something that will raise a smile", said Sir Arnold.

"Here is a poem by Gilbert Keith Chesterton about Noah", said the nurse, "I came across it in a periodical that was left in the chapel. It's a little irreverent though".

Summer passed and Rupert prepared for his final year at grammar school as the news worsened from Europe. Hitler attacked Poland by both land and air, bombing was ferocious as many were killed or injured in Warsaw and other towns. Sir Arnold gathered all his house staff, gardeners, agent, nurse and nursery nurse as he spoke to them from his chair. He permitted them to listen to the Prime Minister on the wireless as they all stood in silence while the outbreak of World War II was declared. Then Sir Arnold shook hands with the young men, men he had known since birth; the stable hands, cook's assistants and finally his agent.

"We do not know if the war will be quickly resolved or drag on for longer but my thoughts, my prayers and my heart go out to you and all your siblings, offspring and parents." Sir Arnold finished his speech as his household went back to their duties until such time as they were called up. Mr Rufus Cuthbert was wringing his hands and gazing out of the window of the long gallery until his employer asked whatever was amiss.

"Sir Arnold", he exclaimed, almost in tears, "I have a heart condition and cannot fight".

"They will have doctor's that will examine you", answered Sir Arnold, "but if you should be spared then it is the will of God. Thanks be that I will have one male friend left to comfort me when all are gone. Dear Mr Cuthbert do not feel abandoned, there will be others like you and you can serve the war effort in other ways. But stay at Mortymer House for now and we will speak to the Rector as to how best we can support you".

Miss Flotsam stayed behind after the agent had departed then knelt down close to Sir Arnold's chair.

"We can only hope and pray that Rupert returns sound of mind and body", she said, " but we have each other while my role, my life, my service are all at your command". Once again in that rare gesture he put her hand to his lips and then said stoically "well Irene, is it not time for tea?"

Chapter 9

Rupert Enlists

"April 1940 and young mister Rupert celebrates his eighteenth birthday today", said Miss Flotsam to Sally Anne, "old enough to enlist to fight for his country. Sir Arnold will be deeply saddened while the whole house will be routing for him. He leaves for the London train at ten o'clock tomorrow morning and it's a grim, hateful business". Sir Arnold ordered his chauffeur to take Rupert to Thatchford to start out on his long journey to Kent where he would undergo training before finding out where he would be posted abroad with his regiment. The eager, younger man promised to write so his guardian presented him with a small, mahogany escritoire with paper, pen and ink. Miss Flotsam gave Rupert a selection of pocket handkerchiefs which she had carefully embroidered with his monogram then shed tears after the motor car had pulled out of the drive.

Sir Arnold received his first letter from his ward, which was shared with Miss Flotsam, and they learned that Rupert had been posted to the French border with Germany where he was involved in some fierce fighting.

The letter was an attempt at bravado to say that the young soldier had made friends and even met some local people. Sir Arnold realised that Rupert was doing his best to keep morale high but conditions were grim.

Every day the news in the local Thatchford Observer worsened. In May 1940 the papers announced that German forces had set to annihilate Belgium, Holland and then France. Sir Arnold spoke to his nurse of his dreadful fears.

"Rupert writes constantly of the good friends he has made but eventually, towards the end of his letter, he lets slip of the number he has already lost. In an attempt at bravado he says he must have nine lives like a cat but he is up against it all the time. He is hoping to come home on leave in time for Christmas but Miss Flotsam it's a bloody business. I pray every night that he will be restored to us, I hope every morning that we will see him again and I feel now more than ever that he really is as a son to me".

Miss Flotsam held his hand and said sadly "Freddy Toogood has just signed up and will take the London train on Wednesday. Thomas Brakespeare has already left and is posted to North Africa. All our friends are such a long, long way from home and in such mortal danger. Why, I can remember the day that they were both caught scrumping your apples and you spoke to them to say they could have as many as they liked if only they went and asked Cook".

"If Rupert does come home in time for Christmas what can we give him? The larder has only the bare essentials needed to survive and we must all survive. Dearest Irene, what are we to do?"

Irene squeezed his hand then shed a tear before speaking reassuringly. "The housekeeper, Cook and I are going to war time cookery demonstrations at Thatchford electricity showrooms. They are taking place on Friday afternoons as advertised in the Observer. On the menu for this week is how to prepare a rabbit stew from scratch using seasonal vegetables from the kitchen garden".

"God go with you Irene", said Sir Arnold with tears in his eyes. "Our Butler was saying that you can make Christmas pudding with grated carrots. We'll serve up a feast when Mister Rupert comes home and we'll invite his grandparents, the Munros, that way we'll get our rabbit".

"Sir Arnold", his nurse said, delighted that he had cheered so much, "perhaps you could answer Rupert's letter in the same cheerful vein to tell him that a feast awaits him on Christmas Day".

"Irene, I will", so Miss Flotsam left her employer to compose his letter.

That year there was a super abundance of plums in the kitchen gardens at Mortymer House inspiring Sir Arnold to pass his copy of the local newspaper to Miss Flotsam for her to show Cook.

"There's a recipe in the paper for plum butter", he said to his nurse. "It sounds delicious, made with cinnamon, ginger and nutmeg. Irene, do we have such things in the pantry?"

"Sir Arnold I am sure we do, I will speak to Cook and pick the plums myself".

Just a few days later, Sir Arnold took afternoon tea in his drawing room and invited Miss Flotsam to join him. The Butler brought in the cups and saucers, tea pot, hot water and muffins with just a scraping of butter kindly supplied by the Munros. There was also a cut glass dish of Cook's homemade plum butter. Sir Arnold sniffed the dish and exclaimed, "well, I can certainly smell the ginger!" Then they tasted the plum butter and gave it their full approval.

"Mmmh!" Cried Sir Arnold, "it really is good. Irene, did you make this?"

"No, it was made by Cook", she replied, "it really is uncommonly good".

"Shall we finish off the muffins?" Asked her employer, "then I will send our appreciation down to the cook".

"Any news from Mister Rupert?" Miss Flotsam asked.

"Yes indeed", answered Sir Arnold, reaching for the breast pocket of his jacket. "This letter arrived today and he is asking for an advance to pay for his train fare home from London in time for his Christmas leave. It has brought to mind the fact that in less than three years' time he will be coming of age. He will be receiving a full allowance but if we are still at war we may have to defer full celebrations. Also the local paper is advertising an appeal to buy and equip a Spitfire. I need to speak to my bankers but I am confident I can give a generous amount. They are asking everyone to give something so I have asked the Housekeeper to announce the details to my remaining staff. It is an absolutely splendid idea but they need £5,000 which is 100,000 shillings although they are doing wonderfully so far".

Chapter 10

Christmas Ceasefire

The night was so dark and black that Rupert could feel his eyes straining. He could see glimpses of enemy fire on the horizon but all around was cold, dark and wet. Rupert was in charge of a gun and all he could think about was the horror of what he had to do. Somewhere out there was the enemy, how wrong to think of a fellow human being in such terms. He must be just a man, like Rupert, no doubt missing his family and longing for a pint of beer or a cigarette. Nervously Rupert felt in his breast pocket but the packet was empty.

Senior Command had warned them to expect a late night attack. Rupert began to sweat then he heard the noise of enemy fire, they were getting closer. He strained to see as finally he heard the order to fire. Later they told Rupert that he had saved many of his comrades that night. His skill in targeting the enemy as they advanced had reduced the number of Allied casualties in his regiment. But he reasoned to himself that there was little point when so many lay dead and dying, dying in vain, far from home and loved ones.

Rupert had survived to fight on, sustaining a wound to his collar bone where a piece of shrapnel was lodged forever. He decided against mentioning the injury in his letter, if he wrote that down it would only torment the older man, his guardian. Sir Arnold had sustained far worse, thought Rupert, yet remained stoical and courageous. The injury allowed the younger man to obtain home leave for Christmas so he wrote a cheerful letter asking how Dr Shiraz was coping with his patient and applying for some funds for the journey.

Rupert came home for Christmas to learn that his guardian and the household were braced for an attack on their nearest port of Sandmouth. This was a bustling, thriving, busy sort of place where fishermen rubbed shoulders with soldiers and seamen embarking to fight on foreign shores. Rupert had come aboard a Merchant Navy vessel bound for South East Wales and at first the sight of these great blue-grey supply ships had been very frightening. The hold of the ship was extensive, designed to store armoured vehicles, arms and supplies. After eight weary months of fighting for his King and Country, Rupert was now more used to seeing tanks but the camouflaged sea vessels and battleships were especially intimidating and the young soldier was glad to disembark.

"What a ghastly mess", he thought as his train pulled into Thatchford station. Home for just four days and there to greet him was his guardian's elderly chauffeur, organising his kit bag while fighting to keep a stiff, upper lip.

"We have been warned by the Prime Minister himself, speaking on the wireless, to expect bomb attacks from the enemy at various sea ports and they may extend inland. Thatchford itself is ready to evacuate to the air raid shelters should the sirens sound. It is so good to see you my son, but I fear it is just for a short while. I see that your arm is in a sling, what happened Rupert?" Sir Arnold spoke a little gruffly as he was clearly moved. Miss Flotsam stood quietly by, near the windows as she wondered if she should leave the room.

"It's a graze to my collar bone, Sir", said the younger man, "but I will have to return as it is healing well I am told. I hope that I am not a coward but I feel for the conscientious objectors today. For myself I can muscle through, but you Sir have your own battles to face here at Mortymer House. How are you getting on with Dr Shiraz?"

Sir Arnold turned as Miss Flotsam moved to stand by his side.

"With the excellent support of my nurse and the admirable doctor I have been able to rise to my feet then walk slowly, supported by two sticks. I have managed to circumnavigate the formal gardens so we try to do this every day whatever the weather. Ice is of course the one thing that will keep me indoors. But enough of me young man, tell us about your friends and are there any nice French ladies to talk to?"

"We don't have time", exclaimed Rupert and his guardian laughed.

"Well Rupert", said Sir Arnold, "tomorrow is Christmas Day and if our magnificent feast of rabbit stew is interrupted by the bombing we will have to pick out the plaster board then eat the meal cold. We have a shelter at the end of the kitchen garden but it's not been tested yet".

On Christmas morning Miss Flotsam slipped into the breakfast parlour holding a slim package wrapped in tissue paper and tied with string. She was a little nervous but spoke formally to her employer.

"Sir Arnold, I have taken the liberty of purchasing a small gift for you out of my salary. I hope you will pardon the liberty".

Sir Arnold took the package from her as he looked up at her blue eyes. "Why Irene, this is really kind of you, I didn't expect a gift. Clearly I pay you far too much".

They laughed together as he opened the package. "Irene, it's a gramophone record, how utterly wonderful. Now let me see, what music does it feature?" Sir Arnold looked at the sleeve of the record and saw that it was a brand new recording of Holst, "The Planets".

"Thank you Miss Flotsam, this is just what I wanted. Now I am a bachelor not very well versed in the ways of ladies so I have a present for you but it is very mundane. Please accept this postal order for ten shillings to spend on yourself as a recompense for the sore trial of having to take care of me all year long".

"Sir Arnold this is an exciting gift, I am truly grateful".

That Christmas the expected bombs did not fall at Sandmouth and Thatchford breathed a sigh of relief for the time being. The local newspaper was delivered on 27th December and reported that the British Government had organised a ceasefire for Christmas. But as soon as the holiday season was over, fierce fighting resumed as Rupert returned to his posting. He was billeted near a small town at Plas de Noir and walked to the village shop one day to see if he could purchase a notebook to keep as a journal.

Chapter 11

Allies and Axis

Rupert's Christmas present from his guardian was a beautifully bound notebook that he wrote in, whenever he could, sometimes writing poems or making sketches of his comrades. He discovered that he filled the pages all too quickly so he had an hour to spare and filled the time by walking to the local post office and corner shop.

"Bonjour Madame", he said to the Post Mistress. Then he explained in his careful, textbook French, what he needed. The Post Mistress directed him to some paperback, blank books for sale together with loose sheets of paper.

"We have very little Sir", she said, anxious to try out her English.

"This is just what I need", said a pleased Rupert who paid for the book then replaced his cap. As he walked back through the town towards his billet he saw a young lady with a bicycle. It had a punctured tyre which the young lady was doing her best to fix. Rupert paused and again using his best textbook French offered Mam'selle assistance. He was quite used to this particular sort of job he explained but lapsed into English as he chatted to the owner of the bicycle. Soon it was up and running again whilst he learnt that her name was Mam'selle Chenu and she helped out at the local Cafe Fromage.

Katrin Chenu had lived at Plas de Noir all her life and longed to escape. She worked hard at the local school hoping that one day she would be able to teach in Paris. Her parents ran the cafe in the village centre and also had a market stall selling their own cheese. Cafe Fromage drew customers from the surrounding villages and farms, it had been a family business for many years so it was to be expected that Katrin should help out at the weekend from an early age. The young man from England intrigued her, he seemed very different from the local men and she was touched by his desire to try out his French. She was also fascinated by his keeping a journal. Well able to read and write, she yearned to further her education but it was classed as an expensive luxury.

Katrin met Rupert again at the cafe then gradually as her English and his French improved she shared her dreams and aspirations. Rupert plucked up the courage to take her walking and admitted that he admired her for having dreams. He told her that he just wanted to survive the war and see his folks again. They talked about Mortymer House which to Katrin seemed very luxurious. Rupert then explained that with the war effort stringent economies had to be made. The younger male servants and tenants had all been called up so the fields were being tended by the local women. He spoke of the extensions to the kitchen gardens which fed the remaining household as well as many of the older villagers of Feverfew and Rupert went on to say that times were hard indeed while his admired guardian was having to struggle just to walk. Then Rupert's collar bone was declared a cure and he had to return to the Front, leaving Katrin his signet ring as a pledge that he would come and find her on his return. Katrin rarely cried, she went to an empty church near Plas de Noir and thanked God that at least she and Rupert were fighting on the same side.

Corvette - for hunting U-boats

Chapter 12

An Interloper

Summer came, and the German forces were set to annihilate Russia. At Northern France bombing by the British Royal Air Force was heavy and many German U boats, moored at Brest and Lorient, were reported as sunk in Sir Arnold's daily newspaper. German soldiers marched through the village of Plas de Noir and one young man stopped at Cafe Fromage to sharply order a coffee with pastries. Katrin nervously served him as the soldier looked her up and down while eating his croissant. Pierre Chenu, Katrin's father, watched from behind the bar as the younger man tried to engage the young girl in conversation using his broken French.

"You should be in Paris", he said, "you are pretty and could earn good money. Why do you stay in a place like this?"

Katrin said nothing but quietly slipped out of the room whilst her father spoke to the German soldier. Pierre tried to obtain information as to why the guards had suddenly appeared at this out of the way location but the young man was too careful, possibly heading for senior rank and giving nothing away. Pierre offered him wine and cigarettes but he took neither and finally went on his way. Just as he was leaving, Jacques the young lad who did deliveries for them arrived to tell Mam'selle Chenu that a parcel from England was at the post office awaiting her attention.

Katrin put away her apron, hanging it on its hook by the door, then hastened to the village post office where Madame Delmas was holding a neatly wrapped, brown package.

"Open it my dear ", she said, "it feels like a book". Indeed the parcel was from Sir Arnold Chepstow and was a copy of Jayne Eyre by Charlotte Brontë. The kind Baronet had also sent his whole month's chocolate ration with a handwritten letter to introduce himself as Rupert's guardian. Sir Arnold wrote to say he could readily spare the treat and the book may help with Mam'selle Chenu's English.

The German soldier became a regular visitor to the Cafe Fromage and opened up to Katrin just a little by saying his name was Hartmund and he also came from a small village on the outskirts of Leipzig. Katrin tried hard to remain non-committal and unresponsive but he was very friendly, also handsome and very determined to speak with her. He announced that he'd been given a few days leave which he was going to spend with his family.

"I will talk with you again Fraulein", he said almost threateningly but he never returned. A letter from Sir

Arnold gave no information, and Rupert was very careful restricting his letters to poems about the French countryside and cheerful stories of his comrades' misdemeanours. Then the Post Mistress was able to obtain a Paris newspaper that reported heavy Allied bombing over Leipzig. Katrin read and sobbed bitterly for the first time, such a handsome young man that she had almost warmed to as a friend. But then amongst her things she felt the hard metal of Rupert's signet ring and she set off to the nearest town on foot to find a school teacher to help her with her English.

Chapter 13

A Food Revolution

January 1943 and the Thatchford Observer was delivered to Mortymer House. Sir Arnold was in the morning room, anxious to gain news. He had not heard from Rupert for several months and the whole neighbourhood had called at the servants entrance with small gifts of winter vegetables wrapped in scraps of paper containing messages of hope and good will. The newspaper was optimistic in tone but Sir Arnold did not feel encouraged to hope that morning. The Axis was mining Sicilian waters, building defences in Southern France and were said to be expanding shore fortifications in Southern Europe. Sir Arnold called for his nurse to discuss the latest developments as they wondered if Rupert had been moved South to deal with the current threat. The Observer also reported a Gestapo purge in France where several thousand French people were to be arrested before deportation to Germany to prevent their revolt.

"Better news in Russia suggests that the German armies there are in jeopardy and also it is to be hoped that the Allies will join forces to drive Hitler out of Africa. So

Miss Flotsam it's not over yet but perhaps we should pray in good earnest for victory".

"There is a tiny article here to say that a young lady from Thatchford has raised over five pounds for the Aid for Russia fund by selling her poetry", replied Miss Flotsam as she scanned the pages her employer was yet to peruse.

"Here is a photograph of a Thatchford lady being taught how to change a tap washer. Plumbers are thin on the ground in civilian life so there is a course at the Technical College for ladies. Irene, I had better send you and Sally Anne as I am unable to stand without leaning on both sticks. The idea is to fix any leaking taps to save water. I don't know if there is a charge but we will find out".

"Very good Sir Arnold, my late father would be turning in his grave but needs must when the Devil drives. Have you written to Rupert since the last letter you received?"

"Yes Irene but it was back in October and no word has reached me since. I heard from the young lady Mam'selle Chenu back in November but she has not heard from my ward either. Is there any news about Tom Brakespeare or Freddy Toogood?"

"None since the autumn", replied the nurse who then gently suggested a turn in the formal gardens. "Today Sir Arnold, we could go further down the avenue as kind old Mr Toogood has hewn a bench out of a dead tree trunk. It is clear if cold but we will wrap up well. The doctor is due to call next week; it would be exciting to report this extra progress".

"Well Irene, I think that sounds like a capital idea. Then I think we are having carrot soup for lunch after which my agent is coming to speak with me about the state of our park trees. It is not very riveting but he does a good job, helping me keep the Estate in good order as far as we can".

Later that year, as summer came to Feverfew and Scatterton, Miss Flotsam was called to her employer's study where, as was customary, he had been reading the Thatchford Observer.

"Here it reports", he began, "that supplies of dried egg have reached Britain from the United States and Canada. The paper recommends eating this muck as a way of keeping the body healthy and robust. It seems that the foodstuff is available all year round so we can have eggs even when the hens have finished laying for the season".

"Can I take that page and share it with Cook?" Miss Flotsam asked.

"Yes indeed", replied her employer, "there is a recipe on how to make the powder into the equivalent of a boiled egg, you can put it with curry sauce and potatoes, and you can even make it into Scotch eggs. Wow Irene, when was the last time we had Scotch eggs? Have we any sausage meat I wonder?"

Miss Flotsam consulted Mrs Martin the Cook while Martin the Butler took a keen interest.

"We know that the Munros are fattening their pigs but not much meat comes our way", he grumbled, "last year most of it was sent up to the Military Hospital and we only had enough for a few meals".

"Can we use the powdered egg to bake cake?" Miss Flotsam asked the Cook.

"I doubt it", answered Cook, "you see when you bake a cake you beat the egg to get air into the mixture. It's the air that makes the cake rise so I can't see this powdered nonsense making a decent sponge". Cook sniffed discontentedly and passed the newspaper back to Miss Flotsam. Then she spoke again.

"We are owed a ration of sausage meat", she recalled, "as Sir Arnold gave his up to the Brakespeares last month when their Grandpa went down with the pleurisy. So if they haven't forgotten we can have Scotch eggs for sure. In fact", she concluded, "that would work. Thank you Miss Flotsam, our delivery boy has just signed up but young Paul Brakespeare said he would fetch our shopping as he is still too young for National Service".

Martin spoke up as he raised his head from looking at the newspaper article.

"It seems that young Paul is going to be joining the coal delivery business that is a reserved occupation which is a great relief as two other Brakespeare sons are out to war. Also their only daughter Dolly is due to join the Auxiliary Service. She is very capable and may be helping to keep ambulance and fire engines working in London".

Mrs Martin was quite taken by this lengthy communication on the part of her husband and became proud and expansive.

"You know nurse, if I dissolve this new fangled powdered egg into water then whisk it up we may be able to bake it into a cake. But what do we do if it won't rise?"

"One thing we know for sure is that Sir Arnold won't complain", comforted the nurse. "We can serve it with fruit and maybe add some condensed milk. After all, there is extra powdered egg available this month and the price is reduced so it's worth the risk". Then the nurse went back to Sir Arnold to announce they would be having Scotch egg followed by fruit flan.

Chapter 14

Sounds of Rejoicing

On the 8th May 1945, Irene woke to a peculiar noise that she thought was sounding in her head. She put her nose outside the bed covers and listened hard but couldn't tell where this unearthly noise was coming from. Then she noticed that Sally Anne had lit a small fire and the kettle was beginning to sing.

"Sally Anne", Irene called as the maid looked up from preparing cups and saucers. "It's quite warm, do we need a fire?"

"Masters orders", asserted Sally Anne rising to her feet. "The Master wants to climb the stairs in front of the young master who is due home today. Sir Arnold wants a fire in every room and the windows flung open to air the house. Also he wants his old bedroom made up in the East wing on the first floor".

"But Sally Anne dear, this is wonderful news but why is Mister Rupert home so soon and is the doctor here?"

"Nurse, we have won the war in Europe. The Prime Minister will be on the wireless at lunchtime and the doctor is coming straight after breakfast to supervise the Master climbing the stairs".

"Dear Sally Anne, is my uniform starched and ready?"

"Yes Miss, but Master says you're to wear your new best rayon dress to welcome the young master and his fiance".

"Dear, what is that noise across the valley?"

"Why Miss, it's the church bells. The Bishop is visiting Thatchford and the bells are ringing out across the diocese".

"Miss Flotsam", said Sir Arnold as she joined him for breakfast that morning, "today my beloved ward and son Rupert is home from the war bringing his new French fiance. We will picnic in the formal gardens at lunchtime then dine in the principal dining room at seven this evening. I will dress for dinner and will climb or attempt to climb the stairs presently. The good doctor will be joining us for lunch".

"Very good, Sir Arnold," said Miss Flotsam, then she shed tears of joy, turning her face from the breakfast table.

"Irene", said Sir Arnold, holding out his hand, "the housekeeper tells me that the drapes in the Master's chamber are old and worn. Would you help me choose some new colours? I shall always need you and I hope that you will move your sleeping accommodation to the room adjoining mine. May I be selfish enough to go on relying on your kindness and support as Rupert and Katrin embark upon their new life together. Dear Irene, give me a hug".

Irene moved from her chair and slipped her arms around his strong shoulders, pressing her damp cheek against his.

"Arnold", she said, "I will stay with you for as long as you need me and my service is always at your call".

After dinner Sir Arnold took Rupert apart from the ladies to leave them to get to know each other. The two men took brandy on the patio.

"I am not in the position to give you much advice", Sir Arnold told the younger man, "but now that this ghastly war is over in Europe we can start to make some plans. Would you like to take a tour of the grounds to see if you would like to make any improvements?"

As Sir Arnold retired for bed that evening he called for Irene to come and sit beside him and talk of Katrin whom they had both enjoyed meeting.

"Her English is superb", said Irene, "and we have been looking at wedding magazines as we talk over cookery ideas".

"I am not a bit sleepy", said Sir Arnold, "come sit on the bed beside me and tell me why you never married".

"My lovely, kind and caring, strong employer", she said softly as he drew her into his arms, "I love you true".

"Irene, your stalwart care and support has been my prop and mainstay now for twenty five years and more.

The salary I pay you is not large but the benefits I reap from having you near are manifold and often unspoken".

"Darling, darling Arnold", she replied, "to see the power in your legs restored and your strength renewed is salary enough".

"Stay with me tonight and every night. Let's see if we can enjoy the same felicity as other lovers, let's see if we can be man and wife in more than just spirit".

Dr Shiraz called at the house a few weeks later to find his patient deadheading the roses in the formal gardens.

"Did you see Irene?" Sir Arnold asked.

"Yes Sir Arnold. My heartiest congratulations, fatherhood will suit you".

The next morning Irene once again heard the sound of bells ringing across the valley. Sir Arnold greeted her with a kiss then announced the rather shocking news that the Earl of Ramptonshire was flinging back the dust sheets of Lindley Hall.

"They will be our neighbours", said the expectant mother. "But Rupert is now an adult and they have a daughter".

"As English law stands today, she may not inherit the title. Well it's Rupert's choice now, he is of age".

The bells continued to peel out as the Chepstows breakfasted as a family.